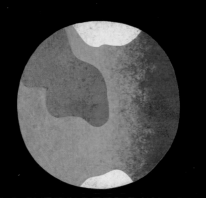

To Kevin: A hearty HUZZAH! for your editorial insight and magical word wizardry

Printed in Malaysia

First Edition

1 3 5 7 9 10 8 6 4 2

H106-9333-5-14105

Library of Congress Cataloging-in-Publication Data

Slack, Michael H., 1969– author, illustrator

Wazdot? / Michael Slack.—First edition.

  pages cm

Summary: An alien is mystified by the sights and sounds of Earth, but a decoder beam helps identify such oddities as a pig, vegetables, and a tractor.

  ISBN 978-1-4231-8347-1 (alk. paper)

[1. Extraterrestrial beings—Fiction. 2. Farms—Fiction. 3. Humorous stories.] I. Title.

PZ7.S628832Waz 2014

[E]—dc23   2013020073

Designed by Tyler Nevins

Text is set in American Typewriter

Art is painted digitally using Adobe Photoshop

Reinforced binding

Visit www.disneyhyperionbooks.com

WAZDOT?

MICHAEL SLACK

Dısney • HYPERION BOOKS

New York

Up.

On top.

PIG!

Leap. Jump. Hop.

Blip, stop!

VEGETABLES!

Blip.

Zot.

Lunch?

Crunch
crop.

CHICKENS!

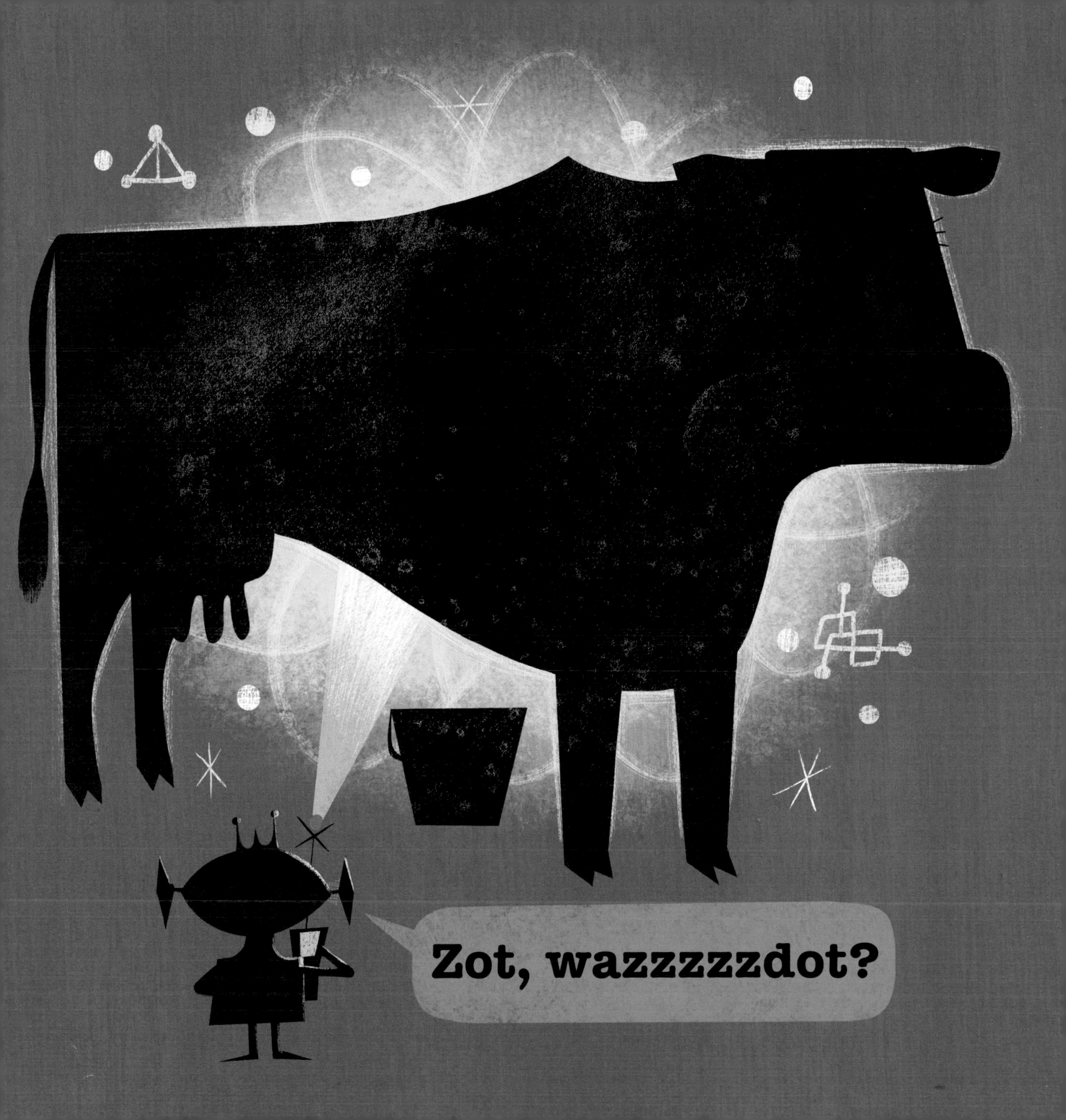
Zot, wazzzzzdot?

COW!

Blip.

Zot.

Drip.
Plip.
Plop.

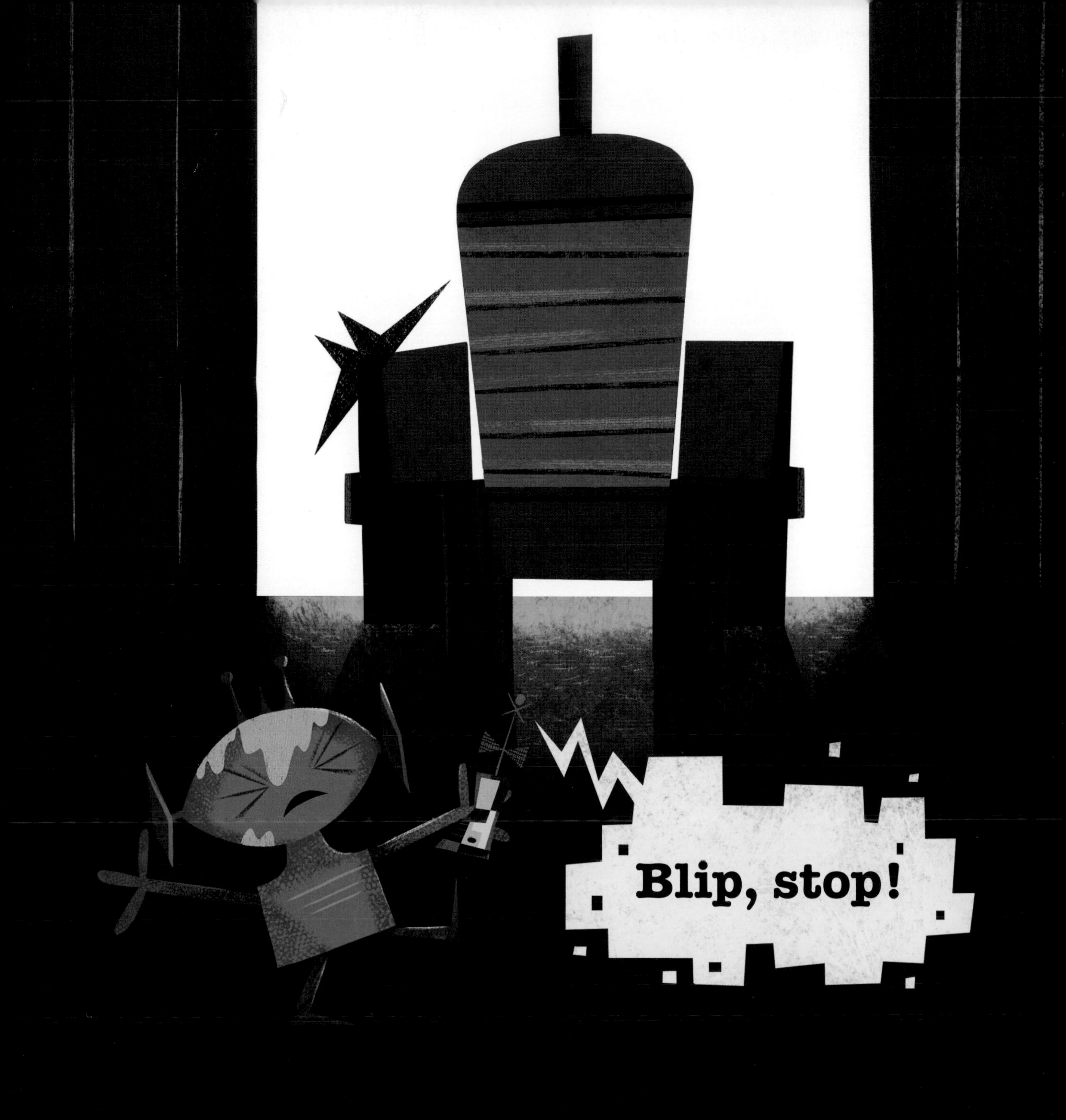
Blip, stop!

TRACTOR!

Blip.
Zot.

Zoom!

Bop!

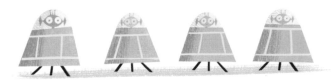

Blip . . .
Zot . . .

wazzzzzdot?

FARM!

Bye-bye!